tate publishing
CHILDREN'S DIVISION

written by:
Paula Guerard

MaryLou
found a
Really
Big S

Published by Tate Publishing & Enterprises, LLC
127 E. Trade Center Terrace | Mustang, Oklahoma 73064 USA
1.888.361.9473 | www.tatepublishing.com

Tate Publishing is committed to excellence in the publishing industry. The company reflects the philosophy established by the founders, based on Psalm 68:11,
"The Lord gave the word and great was the company of those who published it."

Book design copyright © 2014 by Tate Publishing, LLC. All rights reserved.
Cover and interior design by Rhezette Fiel
Illustrations by Kenny Abigae Badana

Published in the United States of America

ISBN: 978-1-63063-360-8
1. Juvenile Fiction / Clothing & Dress
2. Juvenile Fiction / General
14.03.24

This book is dedicated to my parents Joe & Eva Hurley. You may be gone from my sight but not from my heart.

First, I would to thank my husband Mark. He was the push behind me to keep going with the publishing process. Thanks to my children, Mark and Patrice, who read my manuscript and shared lots of great input. To my friend, Joanne Butkiewitcz Foley, I thank you for inspiring me to write a children's book. To my friends and colleagues in the legal field, I thank you for your legal advice and help with editing in the early stages of this project. Last, but certainly not least, to my siblings, Annette, Joe, & Carol, my nieces, nephews, in-laws, cousins, and my friends, which I am blessed with many, I thank you for your love and support.

Marylou Butkiewicz
was playing one day.
Off in the distance she
saw something big far away.

She ran over the hill
and behind a tree.
When she came upon it she
said, "How can that be?"

There in the grass was a giant brown shoe. "My goodness," she said. "Whom could that ever belong to?"

She climbed up the laces to the tippity top.
The shoe was so tall.
She thought she'd never stop.
When she reached the top she said,
"What will I do?"
"I have to do something with
this really big shoe."

All of a sudden
the wind started to wail
The shoe lifted up and
started to sail.

They went over the ocean
and into the sky.
This old broken shoe
knew how to fly!

She peeked out
from over the top.
From there she could see
the local ice cream shop.

She was flying high
over the town.
And was no longer
afraid and enjoyed
looking down.

The shoe picked up speed and
moved even higher from land.
Marylou held onto the laces
with her frail little hands.

She pulled to the left and
then to the right.
Then realized she was steering,
and it was no longer a fright.

This was so much fun and
she wanted to see more.
So she pulled down on the laces
and the shoe started to soar.

Flying over castles
and mountains so high.
Marylou thought
she could touch the sky.

Over the mountains and
big salty sea.
She steered that old shoe and
felt so free.

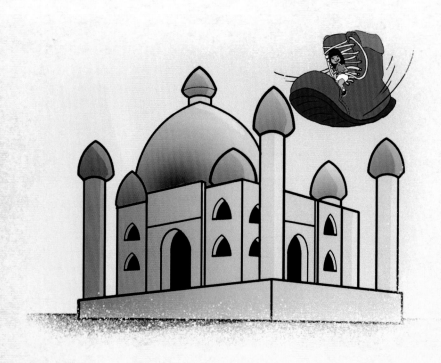

She saw castles and palaces,
beautiful and bright.
This was becoming a spectacular sight.
She realized she was very far from home.
Houses in her town did not
have golden domes.

The pyramids of Egypt
looked like big triangle stones
She called out to the King
sitting on his throne.

She was off then to China
to see the great wall.
Way up so high,
it looked sort of small.

Reaching old England
she waved to the Queen.
This was the most exciting thing
she had ever seen.

In France she cruised by
the Eiffel Tower.
The big clouds above it
caused a rain shower.

Italy was gorgeous
just like in the books.
She could smell pasta and pizza
being prepared by the cooks.

The beautiful Swiss Alps looked
like big candy corns.
She went around again
by the Matterhorn.

Germany's Ale Houses
were filled wall to wall.
People were dancing
on tables in every hall.

Ireland was so beautiful and
green of every tone.
Marylou blew a kiss
to the Blarney Stone.

New Zealand and Australia
were beautiful too.
Marylou steered a little lower
and passed a kangaroo.

She went by Japan
just for kicks.
A man cooking rice
tossed her a pair of
chop sticks.

Into the African
jungle she flew.
"Wow. There are
way more animals
than at the zoo!"

She reached the beaches of Hawaii
where her eyes were glued.
She was racing side by side
with a surfer dude.

She traveled the world in
that big old brown shoe.
From country to country,
she flew and flew.
The trip was exciting,
but it was time to head home.
"Which way will I go?
How far did I roam?"

She held both the laces
tight in her hand.
The shoe soared up over the ocean,
and back over the land.
Going faster and faster
with a hippity hop
Before she knew it, she was back
over the local ice cream shop.

She flew down past the village,
and now safely on land.
Marylou had an adventure
that was ever so grand.

She climbed down from the shoe, and
turned to wave good-bye.
By then, the big old shoe was already
back in the sky.

As the shoe took off for it's next
whimsical trip,
Marylou said, "I wonder if that shoe
can sail like a ship?"

 **e|LIVE**

listen|imagine|view|experience

AUDIO BOOK DOWNLOAD INCLUDED WITH THIS BOOK!

In your hands you hold a complete digital entertainment package. In addition to the paper version, you receive a free download of the audio version of this book. Simply use the code listed below when visiting our website. Once downloaded to your computer, you can listen to the book through your computer's speakers, burn it to an audio CD or save the file to your portable music device (such as Apple's popular iPod) and listen on the go!

How to get your free audio book digital download:

1. Visit www.tatepublishing.com and click on the e|LIVE logo on the home page.
2. Enter the following coupon code:
   da85-fe12-0cb3-960e-c873-48c8-b39d-6fec
3. Download the audio book from your e|LIVE digital locker and begin enjoying your new digital entertainment package today!